Jon Scieszka's TRUCKTOWN
on Reading Street

Mud Fun

Glenview, Illinois • Boston, Massachusetts • Chandler, Arizona
Shoreview, Minnesota • Upper Saddle River, New Jersey

Man, is it wet.
Look at the mud.

Some trucks like mud.

But not Rita.

Mud is not fun for Rita.

3

Will Melvin jump in the mud?

No!

Mud is not fun for Melvin.

Will Jack jump in the mud?

Yes!

Mud is fun for Jack.

Jack will get Max.

Max will get Gabriella.

Will they go in the mud?

Yes! They run in mud.

Yes! They jump in mud.

Yes! They have fun in mud!

Rita and Melvin do not like mud.
Jack, and Max, and Gabriella do!